Working On My Novel

Working On My Novel

Cory Arcangel

PENGUIN BOOKS

PENGUIN BOOKS

Published by the Penguin Group
Penguin Books Ltd, 80 Strand, London WC2R ORL, England
Penguin Group (USA) Inc., 375 Hudson Street, New York, New York 10014, USA
Penguin Group (Canada), 90 Eglinton Avenue East, Suite 700, Toronto, Ontario, Canada M4P 2Y3
(a division of Pearson Penguin Canada Inc.)
Penguin Ireland, 25 St Stephen's Green, Dublin 2, Ireland (a division of Penguin Books Ltd)
Penguin Group (Australia), 707 Collins Street, Melbourne, Victoria 3008, Australia
(a division of Pearson Australia Group Pty Ltd)
Penguin Books India Pvt Ltd, 11 Community Centre, Panchsheel Park, New Delhi – 110 017, India
Penguin Group (NZ), 67 Apollo Drive, Rosedale, Auckland 0632, New Zealand
(a division of Pearson New Zealand Ltd)
Penguin Books (South Africa) (Pty) Ltd, Block D, Rosebank Office Park,
181 Jan Smuts Avenue, Parktown North, Gauteng 2193, South Africa

Penguin Books Ltd, Registered Offices: 80 Strand, London WC2R ORL, England

www.penguin.com

First published in Penguin Books 2014
001

Copyright © Cory Arcangel, 2014

The moral right of the author has been asserted

Set in 18.2/21 pt Georgia
Typeset by Jouve (UK), Milton Keynes
Printed in Great Britain by Clays Ltd, St Ives plc

A CIP catalogue record for this book is available from the British Library

ISBN: 978–1–846–14742–5

www.greenpenguin.co.uk

MIX
Paper from
responsible sources
FSC
www.fsc.org   FSC™ C018179

Penguin Books is committed to a sustainable
future for our business, our readers and our planet.
This book is made from Forest Stewardship
Council™ certified paper.

Working On My Novel

Now that I have a great domain
name I can start working on my
novel

Chris Blow – 7:41 PM – 7 Aug 12

When I'm not studying or working on my novel: I read 50 Shades Of Gray, Watch HBO or Showtime, chill with friends or go party hard #Life<3

Deenie – 10:28 PM – 18 Sep 12

working on my novel but Garth Brooks Live From Vegas is coming back on TV. . . . Nothing will be done the next two hours

Crystal Titus – 9:00 PM – 27 Dec 13

working on my novel for the first time in forever

John Linn – 8:54 PM – 18 Sep 12

Having way too much fun on Pinterest . . . should be working on my novel.

E. Griffin-Isabelle – 11:44 PM – 9 Apr 12

and once i get done watching
doctor who i'm working on my
 novel.

Aeryn B. – 4:12 AM – 24 Mar 12

Chillin by the water working on my novel ..... yup #TheGoodLife

Treasurecarelli – 7:29 PM – 14 Jun 12

Working on my novel, drinking mimosas and laying out by the pool. Good thing I skipped work today! #writing

JD Bourke – 3:14 PM – 15 Jun 12

Working on my novel in a Mexican restaurant with the help of the rain outside the window and a free margarita from the bartender. #writing

Shannon Young – 3:03 AM – 13 Jun 12

Red wine, Einaudi & working on my novel, the ingredients for a blissful night/morning #iamwriting

Helen Churchill – 8:17 PM – 1 Jan 12

Listening to Fleetwood Mac while working on my novel inside the warmth. Yep. Good way to make the most of a rainy day.

BACairns – 7:01 AM – 1 Oct 12

Working on my novel while watching the 25th anniversary phantom of the opera on PBS.

Zack Barnes – 8:40 PM – 11 Mar 12

Working on my Novel and
watching Scary movies :)

Donell jackson – 11:17 PM – 2 Oct 12

Lazy weekend of fantasy football playoffs and working on my novel

Wanna Scribble – 8:36 PM – 17 Dec 11

Cooking some sausages, watching football and working on my novel #GoodSunday

Zandie Thornton – 9:35 AM – 26 Aug 12

Very much enjoying the hubbys
mini vacation. Working on my
Novel as well.

Gwen Selix – 6:17 AM – 15 Nov 12

Sitting at McDonald's working on my novel while Stu does some more electrical work on the RV. Up to 52,500 words now.

Donna B. McNicol – 2:59 PM – 28 Aug 12

Working on my novel and planning our mountain getaway for this weekend. Life's good :)

Lia Oxanne – 4:45 AM – 28 Aug 12

I'm going to spend the next week diligently working on my novel and reevaluating some of my most fundamental beliefs.

Drew Neumann – 11:25 PM – 16 Aug 12

Thinking of starting working on my novel again. But getting my priorities straight first. Job, saving, and the move to Oregon. Priorities.

Marie J Gaddis, can – 11:48 PM – 25 Jul 12

Well, I gave in to temptation and poured a big glass of wine while working on my novel. Now too tired and buzzy to keep writing. Sigh.

Jason Sanford – 10:42 PM – 15 Sep 12

// – Working on my novel and watching Family Guy. Oh yeah!!

Monique J. Pacheco – 7:04 AM – 14 Jun 12

My favorite pass time working on my novel at @BNBuzz (aka Barns N Nobles) while drinking a cup of coffee #purebliss :)

Chelsea Nine – 4:17 PM – 10 Jan 12

Bagel Bites and a nice quiet room is the perfect combination to continue working on my novel :P

James Lanham – 12:07 AM – 25 Feb 12

I'm planning on moving to London to open my own gluten free bakery, but at the moment I'm just kind of laying low and working on my novel.

Haley Sudduth – 12:11 AM – 15 Nov 12

what my break is going to consist of: working on my novel, sleep and netflix

rebecca kuran – 5:55 PM – 21 Dec 12

James Dean shirt on, Arctic Monkeys playing, and working on my novel. According to Goldilocks, I am the picture of a hipster right now. FML

Tonianne Bellomo – 5:41 PM – 17 Aug 12

Working on my novel. It's raining like hell. I love it when it rains & I have time on my side. Maybe I'll sketch at The Met later. #amwritng

Nigia – 8:56 AM – 28 Sep 12

Coffee brewing, check. Gilmore Girls on TV, check. Working on my novel, check! Gotta finish . . . #amwriting

Elizabeth Eileen – 11:38 AM – 29 Dec 11

Strawberry Banana Smoothie and Classic Rewind on Sirius XM . . . Working on my Novel some more. :)

Shane – 12:59 PM – 14 Apr 12

Sitting in Panera, working on my novel. Stop in and say hi!

Don Johansen – 4:17 PM – 5 Jul 12

Sitting at Panera working on my novel. Got a meeting later about the new single. #IndieConnect meeting tonight!

Naima Johnston Bush – 12:20 PM – 13 Sep 12

That's it, that's it, I'm getting off Twitter and working on my novel. Right after I finish this episode of Are You Afraid of the Dark.

Emily Kellogg – 11:21 PM – 12 Jun 12

another useless fact about me on twitter: it's 12:26am and I'm watching Monk and working on my novel and eating cereal.

abby – 2:27 AM – 25 Jul 12

That espresso at ten pm was a bad idea! Listening to Anberlin and working on my novel. Breeze and smells courtesy of the fall rain. #lateni . . .

Hope Alcocer – 3:01 AM – 6 Sep 12

No rest for the wicked. Working on my novel again. Insomnia has its perks.

Connie Ashpol – 8:16 PM – 26 Jul 12

Is it sad that I can't wait until morning so I can start working on my novel again? X

Suzie Tullett – 5:28 PM – 12 Jun 12

Working on my novel tonight
and wondering if I somehow
missed the summer..?

The Scriptwriter – 2:37 PM – 12 Jun 12

I haven't been tweeting much of late, don't worry just working on my novel, eating pasta and reading East of Eden, not dead yet

Pengelife – 12:14 PM – 17 Jul 12

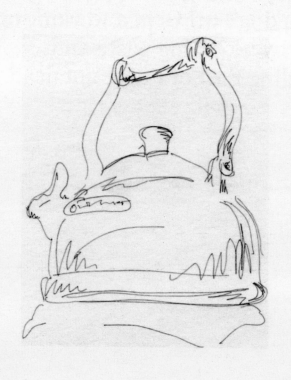

Today was a good day. Now I'm drinking Earl Grey and working on my novel.

Alli Rense Treman – 11:32 PM – 25 May 13

Working on my novel about a dream researcher who .. you'll have to read the book to read what he does!

Monique Berry – 1:16 PM – 12 May 12

Working on my novel while my hair is setting, things are getting biblical.

Air Eater Ⓥ – 10:00 AM – 29 Jul 12

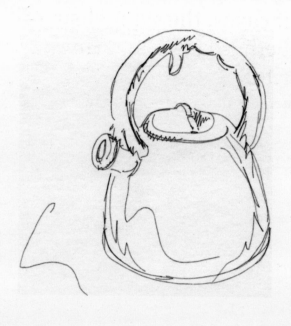

With just one hour of working on my novel I learned stuff about caves, the symbolism of Macbeth's dagger and (my favorite)

Milla van der Have – 2:11 PM – 20 Aug 12

Eating fresh pineapple and working on my novel . . . . a day in the life of a Caribbean writer! hehe

Joana James — 11:35 AM — 16 Jun 12

I want to be in Paris, at the cafe,
working on my novel.

Angela N. Hunt – 4:41 PM – 7 Aug 12

My self summary: just working on my novel

jackson whatever – 1:43 PM – 14 Aug 12

Hanging out in a cafe, just working on my novel.

Ryan David Muirhead – 8:03 PM – 8 Jun 12

#Offline, working on my novel! =) Be back later!

♔ Barblieber ♔ – 3:55 PM – 16 Aug 12

yes I'm working on my novel. I would say I'm around 20–25% complete!

Tear – bear™ – 2:47 PM – 21 Apr 12

Working on my novel . . .

tony summerfelt – 4:19 PM – 9 Mar 13

Working on my #novel

Kyndra – 5:23 PM – 21 Mar 13

working on my novel >>>

Obito – 5:31 PM – 26 Jun 12

Working on my novel

Cory Arcangel – 9:05 AM – 12 Sep 13

Working on my novel

Tiffany Am'rissa – 8:32 AM – 19 Jun 12

Working on my novel ☻

Sam Robertson – 8:49 PM – 2 Jan 13

Working on my novel and screenplay.

Josh Hains – 4:02 PM – 19 Jul 12

Working on my novel :)

PARAMOREquotes – 12:27 AM – 10 Oct 12

Working on my novel :)

Geywalin MeeN L – 12:16 PM – 12 Aug 12

I'm so glad that I'm not working
on my novel.

the_dza – 12:47 AM – 17 Jul 12

Working on my novel again.

Richard MacLean – 2:05 PM – 24 Mar 13

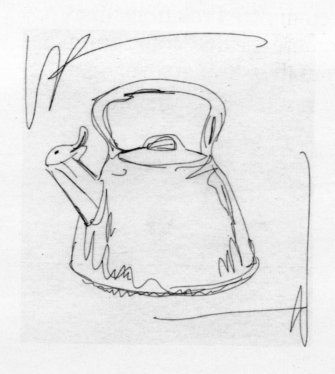

Working on my novel is a lot like a committed relationship; I sometimes take it for granted but fall in love all over again

Shannon – 10:14 PM – 14 Jun 12

The temperature is uncertain today, wanted to ride my bike, might get working on my novel instead.

Robert Allar – 7:29 AM – 24 Jul 12

. . . by working on my novel I mean sitting down with the synopsis and writing "PLOT HOLE!" in red at the end of every other sentence.

Darren Lee – 10:46 AM – 19 Aug 12

Sat in bed working on my novel.
I smell slightly but only allowing
a shower once I've written
another 5 pages. . . .

sassy – 10:56 AM – 12 Jun 12

Laying in bed while listening to some #music and working on my #novel

Sarah Ann – 4:06 AM – 13 Aug 12

I would much rather be working on my novel though. I guess i'll have all summer for that though. Can't wait:)

Pdubber – 3:31 AM – 20 May 13

My love life consists of Nicholas Sparks movie marathons and working on my novel as I write about things that I wish would happen to me. ♥

Monica Medina – 1:25 PM – 8 Dec 12

Working on my novel now,
which apparently has a sense of
discovered structure.

Kate Cannon – 12:42 PM – 27 Jun 12

Tonight, however, I will not be posting. Instead I will be writing the hard words. I'm working on my novel this evening. #wishmeluck

Kelli Stuart – 9:04 PM – 29 May 12

My misery increased when I stopped working on my novel. Hm. . .

Coryl o'Reilly – 8:37 PM – 29 May 12

Working on my novel today about chasing my vineyard dream I have a few chapters so far New Amy MacDonald album is giving some inspiration

Kristina Studzinski – 9:32 AM – 14 Jun 12

Today is the day The day I start working on my novel again The day I stop thinking I can't do it wont get it right The day I believe I can

Maria A Wood – 9:33 AM – 31 May 12

still working on my novel's climax, a battle sequence. . . tricky to get the pacing right

Sean Hannifin – 9:38 AM – 14 Dec 12

Working on my novel while critiquing another. Now that's talent! #amwriting

Diana Long – 10:35 PM – 13 Aug 12

Now working on my novel again hope to get enough Inspiration.#amwriting

Bettina Lippenberger – 9:23 AM – 5 Jun 12

Will be working on my novel
sOon. Perseverance i need
you :-)

Gleizel™ ☺ 29:11 – AM – 21 Sep 12

Should be working on my novel but I'm stuck in the quicksand of a blog entry I'll probably never post anyway.

Kurtis Scaletta – 12:33 PM – 3 Jul 12

Working on my novel. Damn, I got writers' block. –___–

CHA – 6:34 AM – 20 Aug 12

If I continue to work at the
2,000 words a day pace, I'm
going to be working on my novel
forever.

Morgan – 8:42 PM – 10 Jun 12

I know I should continue
working on my novel but I feel
like my laziness just suffocated
any desire I have of sitting and
writing patiently.

Σℓινιαβστясσ . – 8:32 PM – 19 Jul 12

Been working on my novel all morning, my brain is fried. Ughh I have no clue when it's going to be finished

jenn – 3:31 PM – 1 Aug 12

In the span of four hours at the coffee shop working on my novel, I managed to change the word "aloof" to "stuck-up."

James Yeh – 1:06 PM – 26 Jun 12

Going off the grid – need a night to decompress after staring at Excel all day and then coming home and working on my novel #tired

Erin, Creative Soul in Motion – 7:54 PM – 14 Aug 12

I've been working on my novel all day – in between helping customers of course.

TheBrianLennonShow – 5:37 PM – 14 Jul 12

I should have been working on my novel over the last eighteen years. Instead I've been killing zombies and eating pizza. Life = Wasted

Omar – 2:41 PM – 2 Jul 12

I should be working on my novel, but I have bills to pay. #realworldproblems #lifesucks #whyaminotwriting

Stephenie Generose – 12:05 PM – 20 Sep 12

THAT'S WHY I'M WORKING ON MY NOVEL SO I WON'T FEEL SO PATHETIC ANYMORE.

Lucila Morales ;) – 12:46 AM – 30 Jul 12

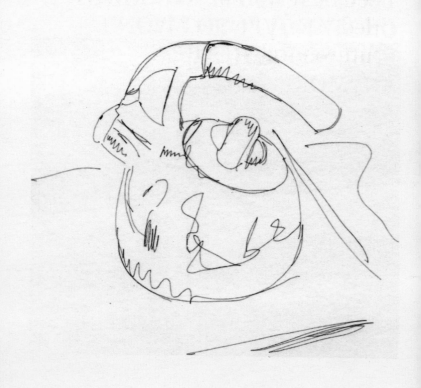

Been busy working on my novel titled "Don't Forget Me". #futurenovelist

Valerie M. Haag – 11:24 PM – 29 May 12

Currently working on my novel and listen to really nice music. Yeah I'm a writer deal with it.

Sierra Brown – 1:25 AM – 1 Dec 12

I'm working on my novel again, and it feels good, you guys. I love my mind.

Stephen Mangol – 11:44 PM – 23 Sep 12

Working on my novel . . . Yea they gone turn this one into a movie

Jasmine Tierra Griggs – 12:33 AM – 23 Jul 12

I'm on a roll. I've written two blog posts tonight, am thinking about a third, a journal post, and working on my novel. O_o

Samantha Owens – 2:22 AM – 12 Aug 12

enjoying working on my novel, it's like i get to vent & let out my fantasy world . . .

Only Pinky . . . – 2:17 AM – 25 Jul 12

Working on my novel . . . a story that will trigger the imagination and offer hope even if it takes a lifetime.

Mary Robertson – 8:07 PM – 30 Jun 12

You think reding adventure books is addicting? Trying writing one :P been working on my novel for 5 hours straight today :) #passionate

White Crayon – 7:16 PM – 2 Jan 12

Finally working on my novel #dedication

★ Nicole ★ – 11:50 PM – 16 Dec 12

Did I mention that I had been working on my #novel for 9–10 hours straight? Yeah, I think that should be mentioned.

Victoria Shayne – 12:07 PM – 14 Aug 12

Time to finish working on my novel! I have a new concept that I really want to work on.

Panda Ninja – 11:26 PM – 5 Jun 12

I just past 24,000 words while working on my novel. Here is to 25,000 before going to paint.

Rebecca Nipper – 4:49 PM – 26 Aug 12

90 minutes working on my novel before 7am! Now its time for a morning walk with the fiance! I finally feel like a #morningperson again.

Nicole Lee – 7:09 AM – 3 Jul 12

Working on my novel. Have now cut it down from 350 pages to 25. Ahh . . . spring cleaning!

Caitlin Baer – 6:42 PM – 6 Jun 12

I finally got back to working on my novel again, after months of being blocked. The results weren't good, but can be rewritten!

Bodhipaksa – 11:43 PM – 2 Dec 12

Working on my novel, #StepSisters. The ideas are just flowing!

#Barblieber♥ – 3:10 PM – 14 Aug 12

BEST day working on my novel on the banks of Lake Tahoe. Perfect weather, words were flowing, and I've knocked out 3 chapters so far!

Stephanie Casher – 10:27 PM – 2 Jun 12

Grooving to Trance Thursday on @diradio and working on my novel. Cheers!

Alannalp – 1:03 PM – 23 Aug 12

Working on my Novel and having fun with it!

Rosalyn – 12:36 PM – 9 Jun 12

I guess not working on my novel for a few days works for me cuz once I begin again I dominate!

Raymond Herrera – 8:40 PM – 1 Dec 13

I'm working on my novel, and it feels amazing.

Aubree – 7:54 PM – 3 Jun 12

After an impressively long power nap, I am working on my novel again. Looks like it's taking shape!

Dutty Bookman – 2:29 AM – 10 Jun 12

For those wondering, i am still working on my novel. I put in 7 hours today and am planning a full day tomorrow. Follow along on #facebook !

Effie Orfanides – 12:17 AM – 14 Sep 12

Eeee!! Alien:resurrection is on. .
But I should be working on my
novel. . Crap!

Niroshehaa – 4:47 PM – 1 Aug 12

I have no beer. What will I drink while working on my novel tonight? #fb

Richard S. Crawford – 12:06 AM – 6 Jun 12

Gonna be up late 2nite working on my novel/drinking by myself first time I've been inspired in awhile #absolut # not an ad

DovinVespa – 1:55 AM – 4 Jun 12

Gotten one hour of working on my novel in, aiming for another before its #timeforwine.

Charlotte R Dixon – 7:18 PM – 6 Jul 12

Working on my novel on Esau
Scrip. I'm looking at you
@HarperCollins

Joel L. Watts – 8:32 PM – 11 Jul 12

I should be studying for finals, but instead I'm working on my novel. Because yolo.

Matthew – 3:58 PM – 17 Dec 13

Final got back to working on my #novel today. Feels good bro.

Chris Riddell – 5:07 PM – 29 Sep 12

Sources

Every effort has been made to credit the authors of these tweets. Please contact the publishers with any corrections.

p.1   https://twitter.com/unthinkingly/statuses/232984923017981953
p.2   https://twitter.com/DinaCzerepak/statuses/248247253033164800
p.3   https://twitter.com/CrystalT_15/status/416750589326815232
p.4   http://twitter.com/johnald90/statuses/248223487607586817
p.5   https://twitter.com/BeedleDee/status/189559467258544128
p.6   https://twitter.com/jiangyin/status/183466217502281728
p.8   https://twitter.com/treasurecarelli/status/213412801220329472
p.9   http://twitter.com/JDBOURKE/statuses/213710992201363457
p.10   https://twitter.com/ShannonYoungHK/status/212802442293821441
p.11   https://twitter.com/HelenChurchill/status/153646160681238528
p.12   https://twitter.com/BeckyACairns/status/252724856636964865
p.13   https://twitter.com/zbarnes/status/179003945488879616
p.14   https://twitter.com/Donelljackson/status/253332814483832832
p.15   https://twitter.com/wannascribble/status/148215082449506309
p.16   https://twitter.com/AlmostTHOR_/status/239717733057572864
p.17   https://twitter.com/GwenSelix/status/269036320310054912
p.18   https://twitter.com/DBMcNicol/status/240524072474255360
        (Donna would love you to visit http://donnamcnicol.com)
p.19   https://twitter.com/Lia_Oxanne/statuses/240369415588311040
p.21   https://twitter.com/DrewNeumann/statuses/236302763380838400
p.22   https://twitter.com/mjgaddis/status/228335988399824896
p.23   https://twitter.com/jasonsanford/status/247163582083633152
p.25   https://twitter.com/MoniqueJPacheco/status/213225453203365888
p.26   https://twitter.com/ChelseaJo9/status/156847204961759232
p.27   https://twitter.com/JaLanham/status/173272795885735936
p.28   https://twitter.com/_haleysudduth/status/268944383397732355
p.30   https://twitter.com/RebeccaGawo/status/282258126424637440
p.31   https://twitter.com/_tonibell/statuses/236578509848469506
p.32   https://twitter.com/Nigia/statuses/251666708794847234

p.33 https://twitter.com/LizEileenwrites/status/152428216966057984
p.34 https://twitter.com/wlftrax/status/191209095410356224
p.35 https://twitter.com/DonBrohansen/statuses/220974692159328257
p.36 https://twitter.com/NaimaJohnston/status/246282278056116226
p.37 https://twitter.com/emily_kellogg/statuses/212746445038690304
p.38 https://twitter.com/abbymoreland/status/228013487274749953
p.39 https://twitter.com/hopealcocer/statuses/243604804650299393
p.40 https://twitter.com/connie_ashpole/statuses/228644994293047296
p.41 https://twitter.com/SuzieTullett/statuses/212657696548204544
p.42 https://twitter.com/DomCarver/statuses/212614712880406528
p.43 https://twitter.com/PeterHayhoePoet/statuses/225262222451032064
p.45 https://twitter.com/allirense/statuses/338497771604676608
p.46 https://twitter.com/1websurfer/status/201360184868749312 (Monique
     would like to include a link to http://halcyonmagazine.blogspot.ca)
p.47 https://twitter.com/LidiaLF/status/229577164155154433
p.49 https://twitter.com/millavdh/statuses/237612839303528448
p.50 https://twitter.com/joana_james/statuses/214018417135595524
p.51 https://twitter.com/angela_n_hunt/status/232939526467747840
p.53 https://twitter.com/jacksonwhatever/statuses/235431353632583680
p.54 https://twitter.com/RyanDavMuirhead/status/211247051390988289
p.55 https://twitter.com/QueenMinaj_xoxo/status/236189409614102528
p.56 https://twitter.com/theredgentleman/status/193773030651072513
p.57 https://twitter.com/snowzone/statuses/310500171031121920
p.58 https://twitter.com/KAKodiak/statuses/314849667760414720
p.59 https://twitter.com/ChambaCat/statuses/217731890600357888
p.60 https://twitter.com/cory_arcangel/status/378142303472197632
p.61 https://twitter.com/Snowdroid1331/statuses/215059418096734208
p.62 https://twitter.com/samr325/statuses/286650508075233283
p.63 https://twitter.com/The_Fighter23/statuses/226044399694528512
p.64 https://twitter.com/PARAMOREquote/statuses/255887308035866624
p.65 https://twitter.com/meengeywalin/status/234684802282967040
p.66 https://twitter.com/the_dza/statuses/225089229783441408
p.67 https://twitter.com/RichardMacLean/statuses/315887177718444035
p.69 https://twitter.com/shannontrimm/status/213454353518960640
p.71 https://twitter.com/RAphotograpy/statuses/227727164563415040
p.72 https://twitter.com/DarrenLeeTwit/statuses/237198862207578114
p.73 https ://twitter.com/sassylapdancer/statuses/212558968965447680
p.74 https://ftwitter.com/xImmortalxAngel/statusl234923837333053440
p.75 https://ft witter.comA/ampyLiar/statuses/336383573126950912
p.76 https://ftwitter.com/ohhlittlemonica/status/277479069405290497
p.77 https://ftwitter.com/KateCannon73/status/218021376714485760
p.79 https://ftwitter.com/kellistuart/statuses/207638495995454400

p.80   https://twitter.com/coryldork/statuses/207631802897137666
p.81   https:/ftwitter.com/KristinaStud/status/21326251765125120O
p.82   https:/ftwitter.comlArtfulHelix/statuses/208189478609756160
p.83   https://twitter.com/seanthebest/status/279596200070627328
p.84   https://twitter.com/dianalong87/statuses/235203005278978048
p.85   https://twitter.com/wavedancer74/status/209998845457858560
p.86   https://twitter.com/secretzel/statuses/249168393851269121
p.87   https://twitter.com/kurtisscaletta/statuses/220193552045588481
p.88   https://twitter.com/Chaaaaaarisse/status/237497778253725696
p.89   https://twitter.com/WriterMorgan/statuses/211921179148165120
p.90   https://twitter.com/liviixo/status/226112358987202562
p.91   https://twitter.com/jennyferrsofiaa/status/230747514658234369
p.92   https://twitter.com/jamesyeh/status/217665053774712832
p.93   https://twitter.com/IamCre8tiveSoul/statuses/235524947106222080
p.94   https://twitter.com/brianlennonshow/statuses/224256384672342016
p.95   https://twitter.com/OmarBromarMkVII/statuses/219863352552325120
p.96   https://twitter.com/Generoses13/statuses/248815167704535040
p.97   https://twitter.com/UndesiredCaress/status/229800134823796736
p.99   https://twitter.com/valeriemhaag/statuses/207673747312881666
p.100   https://twitter.com/SoulAlexis135/status/274761115819458560
p.101   https://twitter.com/Swmangol/status/250078253686091776
p.102   https://twitter.com/Amazing_Tierra/status/227260150241714177
p.103   https://twitter.com/sowensphoto/status/234535260858249216
p.104   https://twitter.com/shesah_KEEper/statuses/228011054989451264
p.105   https://twitter.com/maggiesraggedy/status/219220568615030784
p.106   https://twitter.com/sarahcollie49/status/153992988626915328
p.107   https://twitter.com/nfizzle94/status/280535483723964417
p.108   https://twitter.com/ThyNameIsTori/status/235407183263711232
p.109   https://twitter.com/brittney_canna/status/210211104851378176
p.110   https://twitter.com/RebeccaNipper/statuses/239826983406686208
p.111   https://twitter.com/NicoleJMU09/status/2201120366994554488
p.112   https://twitter.com/CaitlinJBaer/statuses/210501940596051968
p.113   https://twitter.com/Bodhipaksa/status/275460229313994752
p.114   https://twitter.com/QueenBarblieber/status/235453378665263104
p.115   https://twitter.com/stephcasher/status/209109017199517697
p.116   https://twitter.com/alannalp/statuses/238682988819386368
p.117   https://twitter.com/blessednowF/status/211496922047975427
p.118   https://twitter.com/rayy_rayyy/status/407323457076998144
p.119   https://twitter.com/breeOGRAPHY/status/209432832848838656
p.120   https://twitter.com/duttyBOOKman/status/211706547565379584
           (Dutty is the author of *Tried & True: Revelations of a Rebellious Youth*)
p.121   https://twitter.com/LegendaryWriter/status/246462657966772224

p.122   https://twitter.com/niroshehaa/statuses/230766789674541056
p.123   https://twitter.com/underpope/statuses/210220972219973633
p.124   https://twitter.com/DovinVespa/statuses/209523748594925571
p.125   https://twitter.com/Wordstrumpet/status/221382551657385985
p.126   https://twitter.com/eJoelWatts/statuses/223213305718767616
p.127   https://twitter.com/PureEvans/status/413050598741655553
p.128   https://twitter.com/CR_Riddell/status/252152616837070850

Acknowledgements

Hanne Mugaas, Arcangel Surfware/Studio, Brooklyn (Amanda Schmidt, Gil Gentile, and Allie Tepper), Familiar Studio, New York (Carl Williamson, Ian Crowther and Keith Mancuso), Helen Conford, Michael Arcangel, Maureen Arcangel, Sable Arcangel, Justin Arcangel, Jessica Arcangel, Jamie Arcangel, Edward Carrigg. In memory: Betty Carrigg.

Cory Arcangel is an American fine artist whose best-known projects include videos of cats on pianos edited to recreate Schoenberg's Three Piano Pieces; a series of hacks of popular video games such as *Super Mario Brothers* without any characters; and Pizza Party, a free software package that could be used to order Domino's pizza through a command-line interface. His work has been exhibited at the Barbican Centre in London, the Museum of Modern Art in New York and the Hamburger Bahnhof in Berlin, and his online work, source code and ephemera are available on his website: http://www.coryarcangel.com. His Twitter feed for *Working on My Novel* can be found at https://twitter.com/WrknOnMyNovel.